The
STORY
of the
THREE
KINGDOMS

The
STORY
of the
THREE
KINGDOMS

BY

Walter Dean Myers

ILLUSTRATED BY

Ashley Bryan

HarperCollins*Publishers*

 Long ago, when the earth had not settled in its turning and the stars had not found their places in the night sky, there were three kingdoms.

The first kingdom was that of the forest, and in the kingdom of the forest the giant Elephant ruled. When he spoke the trees trembled. When he walked the ground shook. No beast, great or small, dared to speak against him. No one would look into his great eye, for they were afraid to hurt his feelings.

"Mine is the greatest kingdom on earth," Elephant was fond of saying.

And as powerful as he was, many believed this to be true.

The second kingdom was that of the sea, and the ruler of the sea was Shark. Shark had many rows of sharp and shiny teeth that he bared in an angry glare. Fish both small and large would swim away when he came near. Lobsters would cover their mouths lest they speak a word that might be misunderstood.

"Mine is the greatest kingdom on earth," Shark would say from his home in the sea.

And since the sea covered most of the earth, many believed this to be true.

The third kingdom was that of the air, that wide place between heaven and earth, and it was Hawk who ruled the air. He soared through the skies each day with a great cry of "KAAAAAAA–AH! Kaaaaaa–AH!" Hawk had a great hooked beak and wickedly curved claws that he held ready as he soared swiftly on the wind.

When he flew, the thrush and the swallow would hide in the bushes.

"Mine is the greatest kingdom on earth," Hawk would call out from the skies. As much space as the sea held, the sky held more. Who was to deny that his kingdom was the greatest?

Elephant, Shark, and Hawk often argued among themselves.

"Come into my forest," said Elephant, "and let us test who is the strongest."

But Hawk and Shark would not go into the forest.

"Come into my sea," called Shark, "and I will teach you to obey me."

But neither Hawk nor Elephant would venture into the sea.

"Come into the air," Hawk cried, "and we will see who is master."

But neither Shark nor Elephant could lift themselves from the ground.

So it went, with each ruler thinking that his was the greatest kingdom and that he ruled the earth.

Then there came to earth some new creatures. They called themselves the People. They were not as strong as Elephant. They were not as fierce as Shark. Nor could they fly, like Hawk.

All of the other creatures in the forest, in the sea, and in the air laughed at the People.

"You are here to do our bidding," they all called out. And so it seemed. For many seasons the People walked with their chins upon their chests and their eyes cast down.

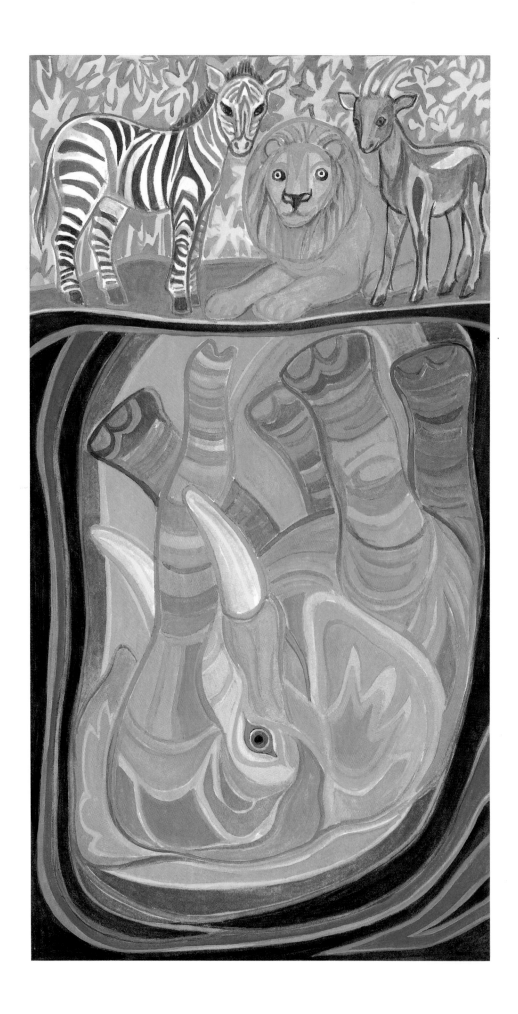

The People lived in the hills, not daring to go into the forest for fear that Elephant would crush them with his great strength.

Then it happened one day that Elephant fell into a great pit. Try as he might, he could not pull himself up. Nor was any other creature strong enough to pull him up. Many thought it was the end of Elephant.

But that night some of the People were sitting around a great fire. One spoke of something he had once seen. There had been a great stone in a place where the People wanted to build a village. The stone was too big for any one of the people to lift. But there were vines around the stone and some of the People pulled on them. With many of the People pulling on the vines the stone moved easily. Then the village was built.

This story was told and told again. The idea warmed in the minds of the People, and they knew it was good. The next day the People went to the pit. They tied many vines around Elephant and pulled him out. Elephant was grateful for their help.

"From this day on I will share the forest with you," said Elephant.

And so he did.

Another time it came to pass that Shark, with his terrible teeth, would not let the People bathe in the sea or take fish for their meals.

The People were sad as they sat around their fire. Then a woman told how her grandmother had woven a mat for her home. One day by chance she dropped it into a small brook. Lizard, swimming by, had caught himself in her weaving and could not escape. The People made the woman tell the story many times. They warmed the idea carefully in their minds, and knew it was good.

The next day the People wove the largest mat they could and threw it into the water. Into the net swam Shark, and he could not move.

"Let me loose!" Shark cried.

"Will you share the sea with us?" asked the People.

Shark turned and squirmed and gnashed his teeth, but he could not free himself from the net the People had woven.

"Let me loose," Shark cried, "and we will share the sea."

The People cut the mat and let Shark swim away. They never feared him again.

But Hawk, with his hooked beak and slashing claws, just laughed as he flew among the clouds.

"I am still ruler of the sky," he called. "And mine is the greatest kingdom!"

The People were afraid of Hawk, and they trembled when he flew above them.

But now the People knew what they could do. They gathered again around the fire and each told the stories they remembered. One told of watching a child trying to catch a butterfly. The child could not catch the butterfly as it flew, but caught it when it came to rest upon the ground.

This story, too, warmed in the minds of the People and they knew the idea was good. The next day the People went to the baobab tree where they knew Hawk came to rest. They waited, and when Hawk landed they threw a loop made from vines around him. Hawk screeched and flapped his wings, but he could not escape.

"Let me go," Hawk cried, "and I will share the air with you."

The People freed Hawk from the vines and no longer feared him.

"Now we are the masters of the earth," cried a young man. "We can rule the forest and make Elephant fear us! We can rule the sea and Shark will flee from us! We can rule the air and Hawk will tremble!"

But when the People gathered once again around the fire, telling the story of all that had happened, something new came to mind.

"We have overcome the strength of Elephant," they said, "and our fear of Shark and Hawk. We have done this by sitting by the fire and telling stories of what has happened to us, and learning from them. Only we, among all creatures, have the gift of story and the wisdom it brings. We do not need to be masters of the earth. We can share because it is wise to do so."

From that day on the People held their heads high, never forgetting to sit by the fire and tell their stories. Never forgetting that in the stories could be found wisdom and in wisdom, strength.

For my sister,
Elaine Martindale
–A. B.

The Story of the Three Kingdoms
Text copyright © 1995 by Walter Dean Myers
Illustrations copyright © 1995 by Ashley Bryan
Printed in the U.S.A. All rights reserved.

Library of Congress Cataloging-in-Publication Data
Myers, Walter Dean, date
  The story of the three kingdoms / by Walter Dean Myers ; illustrated by
Ashley Bryan.
      p.   cm.
  Summary: Long ago, Elephant ruled the forest, Shark ruled the sea, and
Hawk ruled the sky, until People discovered a unique power that enabled them
to dominate the other creatures.
  ISBN 0-06-024286-8. — ISBN 0-06-024287-6 (lib. bdg.)
  [1. Animals—Fiction.   2. Human-animal relationships—Fiction.
3. Storytelling—Fiction.]   I. Bryan, Ashley, ill.   II. Title.
PZ7.M992St   1995   94-2685
[E]–dc20   CIP
                                                                          AC

1   2   3   4   5   6   7   8   9   10
❖
First Edition